Text copyright © 2001 by Joanne Ryder
Illustrations copyright © 2001 by Richard Jesse Watson

First Edition

Published by Sierra Club Books for Children
85 Second Street, San Francisco, California 94105
www.sierraclub.org/books

Published in conjunction with Gibbs Smith, Publisher
P.O. Box 667, Layton, Utah 84041
www.gibbs-smith.com

SIERRA CLUB, SIERRA CLUB BOOKS, and the Sierra Club design logos
are registered trademarks of the Sierra Club.

Library of Congress Cataloging-in-Publication Data
Ryder, Joanne.
    The Waterfall's gift/by Joanne Ryder; illustrated by Richard Jesse Watson.–1st ed.
        p. cm
    Summary: On a visit to the old north woods, a girl enjoys the many natural treasures
hidden in its deepest places.
    ISBN 0-87156-579-X (alk. paper)
    [1. Nature—Fiction.] I. Watson, Richard Jesse, ill. II. Title.
PZ7.R959 Wat 2000
[E]—dc21   99-056157

Art direction by Susan Lu Bussard
Book and jacket design by Rick Halverson
Printed in Hong Kong

10 9 8 7 6 5 4 3 2 1

For Ray Ryder,
who saw treasure everywhere

JR

For me mither, Elsie Martha Grierson MacLeod Watson

Warm thanks to: Helen Sweetland, Rick Halverson, Susan Lu Bussard,
Kevin Streeter, Faith Pray, Mia Baylor, and Nicholas Colitses.

RJW

The Waterfall's Gift

by Joanne Ryder

Illustrated by Richard Jesse Watson

Sierra Club Books for Children

SAN FRANCISCO

When my Grandpa was young,
he built a small cabin in the woods.
Whenever I think of him, he's there,
walking under the tall trees,
gently turning over logs and leaves
to see what's hidden underneath.
"The old north woods hides treasure
in its deepest places," he always told me.

It still does, even though he's gone.
So when the days get long and hot,
my family journeys northward,
each of us treasure seekers,
filling the car, singing old songs.

Tucked between boxes and Grandma,
I watch the hawks circling slowly
over the hills, over the tall trees,
as we ride the smooth dark path
taking us to the old north woods once more.

The road curves this way
and that way till around
the last curve, we see
the small brown house
waiting for us to find it again.

Mama boosts the windows wide,
and we push outside
the thick strong smell of winter.
I write my name in dust and blow
it all away, except the last two letters.
By fall, new dust will fill the spaces.

I hear laughter in Grandma's room, and follow.
"Look," she says softly, as a baby mouse
runs and runs in circles like a toy.
Quietly, we watch it —
so tiny, it slips behind the curtains,
never moving them,
as it finds a small safe hole.
We share the cabin with the small ones
who share the woods with us.

And now, the woods are calling me.
"I'm off!" I shout, as the others
begin exploring old closets and drawers.
Nobody asks me where I'm going,
but Mama finds my warmest sweater.
"It'll be cold there yet," she says.

Greenness stretches across my trail,
but thin leafy arms can't hold me back.
I run on through, making a new path.
At a bright clear spot, I find
Mama's sitting rock, green too.
My fingers brush the furry moss around me,
so new, no one has felt its softness yet.
I dangle my toes above the stream,
guessing if the water is still too, too cold.
I know it is —

            but dip my toes in anyway.
Brrrrr. I rub them pink and warm again.

All around me
there are walls red with berries,
and I pluck one and one and one
till the black bear inside me roars:
More. Give me more.
So I eat a pawful, eat them all.
Well, not quite all!
I save some for Papa,
who likes these berries best.

Somewhere above me, a bird chirps a question.
I click back my answer; she asks me another.
We talk and say so many things. I wonder what?
Click. Click.
I wait —

but this time
no one answers me.

So I fly away, too,
leaping over stones and logs
down the brambly hill.

And as I pass them,
a million green leaves wave around me,
hiding everything except the deep sound
that finds its own way through to greet me.
It is a voice that never fades or changes,
calling me louder as I run nearer, roaring:
NOW, NOW, NOW, NOW, NOW, NOW.

And then I see a patch of moving whiteness
and I am there. The old north woods
hides treasure in its deepest places.

Far above me, there are cliffs
of dark wet rock that almost touch the sky.
From these cliffs the water leaps
downward, tumbling and foaming,
to melt into the wide green pool below.
I listen —
and my waterfall says what it always says:
NOW, NOW, NOW, NOW....

I walk around the deep pool,
Grandpa's special place,
where he knew how to find
the safe path, the steady rocks
to climb. I remember...
and I find my way around.
And just like Grandpa showed me,
I find a smooth white stone
and throw it hard and sure
till it skims and skips and skips
across the moving water —
skipping farther than
I've ever thrown before,
sinking closer to the waterfall,
one perfect stone cast back,
one tiny treasure as my gift.

Then I climb the warm rocks,
sprinkled with sunlight,
finding my own sitting place.
I close my eyes and wait and wish
my summer's wish, until I hear the sound
of small wet paws squeaking and feel
someone has found me.

And she has.
A small wet one, fat like a puppy,
watches me watching her, and lifts
her sleek brown head above the grass
to get a better look. I wonder
what she thinks I am.
I think she is an otter.

And when she's seen enough of me,
she slides into the pool to play.
She dives, then pops up in some unexpected spot,
turning to check if I'm still watching her.
Maybe — some warmer day —
she'll let me swim with her.
I slide from my rock, following her bubbly path
till she disappears downstream,
and, wishing her well, I whisper good-bye.

As the sun hides in the trees, I find the trail.
Yet for the longest time,
the waterfall stays with me, roaring,
until I reach the old dead tree and know
I somewhere stepped across an unseen line
and cannot hear the water's call.
From here on in, I only feel the call of home.

I tiptoe past the hammock with Grandma
sunk inside. But she's not sleeping.
"Doesn't that look like a swan?" she asks,
pointing and sharing her sky with me.
"More like a dragon," I say,
and I stretch out on the grass beside her.
"I saw an otter at the fall, Grandma."
And I hear her draw her breath and say,
"An otter! Oh, you're lucky.
I haven't seen an otter in a long, long time."

And I do feel lucky,
letting the clouds roll by above me,
and feeling summer begin in the old north woods.

The illustrations in this book were painted in egg tempera
on Strathmore illustration board.
The display type was hand-lettered by Faith Pray.
The text type is Bembo.